SUDAN

COUNTRIES IN CRISIS

SEAN CONNOLLY

Rourke
Publishing LLC
Vero Beach, Florida 32964

www.rourkepublishing.com

PHOTO CREDITS: p. 18-19: Bettmann/Corbis; p. 12-13: Robert Caputo/Getty Images; p. 22-23, 31: Eskinder
Debebe/UN Photo; p. 9: Sylvain Grandadam/Getty Images; p. 16: Hulton Archive/Getty Images;
pp. 11, 14, 17, 20: Library of Congress; p. 10: Benjamin Lowy/Corbis; p. 39: Peter Macdiarmid/Getty Images;
p. 25: Francoise de Mulder/Corbis; p. 42: Fred Naz/UN Photo; pp. 7, 36-37: Scott Nelson/Getty Images;
p. 26: Jehad Nga/Corbis; p. 27: Morteza Nikeubazi/Reuters/Corbis; p. 32: Antony Njuguna/Reuters/Corbis;
p. 5: Jean Nordmann/istockphoto.com; p. 29: S. Peterson/Liaison Agency/Getty Images; p. 40: Refugees
International; p. 34: Evan Schneider/UN Photo; p. 41: H.C. Stikkel/U.S. Department of Defense; p. 28: U.S.
Department of Defense; p. 15: Khoo Eng Yow/istockphoto.com.

Cover picture shows homeless Sudanese people, forced to live in refugee camps [Eskinder Debebe/UN Photo].

Produced for Rourke Publishing by Discovery Books
Editors: Geoff Barker, Amy Bauman, James Nixon
Designer: Keith Williams
Photo researcher: Rachel Tisdale

Library of Congress Cataloging-in-Publication Data

Connolly, Sean, 1956-
  Sudan / Sean Connolly.
     p. cm. -- (Countries in crisis)
  Includes index.
  ISBN 978-1-60044-618-4
  1. Sudan--History--Juvenile literature. I. Title.
  DT155.4.C66 2008
  962.4--dc22
                                    2007020679

Printed in the USA

CONTENTS

CHAPTER ONE

Conflict and Hunger

Families struggle across a dry and dusty landscape. Mothers carry tiny babies. Skinny children walk beside them in the dirt. Men carry a few belongings. These families are **refugees**. They have been driven from their villages by armed men riding horses and camels.

Suddenly, a group of men gallops past the walkers. They fire guns as they ride. Several of the refugees fall dead. Others are wounded. Children and babies cry with fear. The men ride off into the darkness.

Hungry people wait patiently for a portion of food aid in Sudan's Darfur region.

SUDAN

This young girl is among the hundreds of thousands of people who have lost their homes because of fighting in Sudan.

WHAT IS A FAMINE?

A big problem facing western Sudan is famine. A famine is more serious—and deadlier—than a food shortage. A famine may last months or even years.

CYCLES OF VIOLENCE

This terrible scene is typical of life in Darfur. Darfur is a region in western Sudan. For more than three years, the people have suffered awful violence. The Sudan government supports the armed riders who sweep into Darfur, destroy villages, and drive people from their homes. Hundreds of thousands of people have died.

Millions have fled. Those who stay in their homes face terrible hunger.

The violence seems to have no end. Sudan's government refuses to let peacekeeping soldiers into Darfur. And all of this is happening in a country that already had nearly fifty years of **civil war**. Darfur's new violence began just as that war finally ended.

LIFE IN DARFUR

> Throughout Darfur. . .villages have been bombed and their inhabitants killed, **raped** and forced into government-run **concentration camps**. . . agencies have been denied access to most of the displaced. Some people, though near starvation, are refusing aid for fear of retribution [punishment].

New York Times Op-Ed page

Cooking pots are all that remain of a burned-out house in the village of Chero Kasi, after armed horsemen attacked in September 2004.

CHAPTER TWO

Old Divisions

Sudan is the largest country in Africa. It is found between **tropical** central Africa and dry North Africa. Most of the country lies on a dry, flat, dusty plain. Mountains rise up in the west and the south. The south is also the wettest part of Sudan. Parts of it are thick rain forest. The Nile River is probably Sudan's most important feature. This is the world's largest river. Two branches of it meet at Khartoum, Sudan's capital.

WHERE IS SUDAN?

EGYPT

LIBYA

SAUDI ARABIA

SUDAN is in Africa

Nile River

Port Sudan

Red Sea

Merowe

Atbara

Omdurman

KHARTOUM

Atbara River

ERITREA

YEMEN

Darfur

Geneina

CHAD

SUDAN

Blue Nile River

Kosti

ETHIOPIA

White Nile River

CENTRAL AFRICAN REPUBLIC

N
W E
S

km
0   300
0   300
miles

Nimule

ZAIRE

UGANDA

KENYA

The Nile River creates a thin fringe of fertile land in a country that is mainly covered by rocky, sandy deserts.

The remains of pyramids that once served as tombs for kings and queens of the ancient kingdom of Meroe, in Nubia (between 300 B.C. and 300 A.D.)

OFTEN DIVIDED

For much of its history, Sudan was not a single country. It was made up of separate kingdoms. Several of the kingdoms grew and traded along the Nile River.

WHO'S WHO IN SUDAN?

Modern Sudan is divided on many matters. These include religion, **ethnic group**, language, and region. Many of the conflicts are tied to the country's north-south divide. Northern Sudan is mainly **Muslim**. It has a large Arab population and a Nubian (non-Arab but Muslim) minority. Nilotic people live in the southern parts of Sudan. (Nilotic describes non-Arab groups sharing some language roots.) These people have not converted to **Islam**. They have traditional African or Christian beliefs.

This photograph from the 19th century shows a Nubian woman wearing traditional clothing and jewelry.

The Nile connected these ancient kingdoms with Egypt. Egypt is Sudan's powerful northern neighbor. This ancient civilization also developed along the Nile. Much of Sudan's history is linked to Egypt. At the time of the Egyptian pharaohs, Sudan was called Nubia, or Kush.

PROLONGED PEACE

The Prophet Muhammad founded Islam. He died in 632 A.D. Islam spread quickly from the Arabian Peninsula to neighboring lands. By 700 A.D., nearly all of North Africa had been conquered by Arabs. The people converted to the Muslim faith.

Things did not go as easily in Nubia. The Arab people were beaten back in 642 and 652. Such losses were unheard of for the Muslim invaders. As a result, they agreed to a treaty with the Nubians. This treaty was known as the baqt. It promised Nubian independence. In exchange, the Nubians paid a **tribute** of slaves each year. The baqt lasted nearly 700 years. It is one of history's longest-lasting treaties.

In the early 1800s, Egypt conquered the area and united it. By that time, most of the Sudanese people were Muslim. But they felt different from the ruling Egyptians. Modern Sudan was born.

The rivers and marshes of the Sudd swell each year after the rainy season.

THE SUDD

Deep in south-central Sudan is a thick swamp. It straddles the Nile and covers more than 11,500 square miles (30,000 sq kilometers). This marsh is called the Sudd. (This means "barrier" in Arabic.) Passing through, either on foot or by boat, is hard. The size of the Sudd depends on how much the Nile floods each rainy season. Throughout history, the Sudd has blocked both explorers and invaders heading south.

CHAPTER THREE

Birth Pains

Many countries have been involved in Sudan's history. The Egyptians controlled much of northern Sudan in the early 1800s. But the Egyptians themselves belonged to the larger Ottoman (Turkish) empire. The government they founded in Sudan in 1821 was called the Turkiyah.

REBELLION AND DEFEAT

The Turkiyah government ruled northern Sudan. The leaders mostly ignored the southern people. But the first moves toward a united, independent Sudan came

A poster from 1897 shows British people in Sudan escaping from the Mahdi's forces.

THE MAHDI OR FOR THE VICTORIA CROSS

SCENE 1st SUNSET IN THE SOUDAN. THE DECLARATION OF HOSTILITIES AND PERSECUTION OF CHRISTIANS BY THE SOUDANESE

THE "SCRAMBLE FOR AFRICA"

European countries had traded with Africa since the sixteenth century. In the nineteenth century, this relationship changed. European powers began colonizing parts of Africa. They saw Africa as a source of raw materials such as rubber, copper, cotton, and tea. It was also a market for their products. The major European powers included Great Britain, France, and Germany. Each wanted to have the most African **colonies**. This was called the "Scramble for Africa."

Colonizers of Africa were interested in tea and many other products.

British troops head for Khartoum in 1885, during Sudanese revolt against Egyptian rule.

from the south. A southern Muslim led a rebellion in 1881. He called himself the Mahdi. Fighting swept into northern Sudan. The Egyptians called on Britain to help.

In 1885, the Mahdi's rebels captured Khartoum. They killed General Charles Gordon, the British army commander there. Sudan declared itself an independent country.

COLONIAL DIVISIONS

The British trained people to help them run Sudan. Local people handled minor government jobs. To help educate the people, the British opened Gordon Memorial College in Khartoum in 1902. Most of the college's students came from the Muslim and Arabic-speaking north of Sudan.

Gordon Memorial College trained men from northern Sudan for important jobs in their country.

In 1896, Britain and Egypt struck back. British soldiers pushed south into Sudan. They captured towns along the way. By 1898, they met with a Sudanese army at Omdurman. This is near Khartoum. The British and Egyptian soldiers were outnumbered. But the British had modern weapons such as cannons and machine guns. In the Battle of Omdurman, nearly 10,000 Sudanese soldiers died. Only 48 British and Egyptians died.

By 1898, the British had sent enough troops and modern weapons to defeat the Sudanese rebels easily.

A photo from around 1905 shows a Sudanese soldier serving in the British army.

ANGLO-EGYPTIAN SUDAN

After Omdurman, Sudan was ruled jointly by Great Britain and Egypt. The territory was called Anglo-Egyptian Sudan. It flew both British and Egyptian flags. And Egypt, with British support, chose a governor-general. But, in reality, Sudan was a British colony.

By the twentieth century, the British had the largest empire in the world. But the British needed people to govern the empire's many regions and districts. They relied on local people to help run things.

For fifty years, Sudanese young people were educated in the British style. They then governed much of Anglo-Egyptian Sudan. By the early 1950s, though, many African and Asian colonies were pushing for independence.

INDEPENDENCE WITHOUT UNITY

In 1953, the United Kingdom and Egypt were planning for Sudanese independence. It would take three years. In 1954, Sudanese voters elected a new **parliament**. Ismail al-Aihiri, leader of the National Unionist Party, became Sudan's first prime minister. In December 1955, the Sudanese parliament voted for complete independence.

The new country had a shaky start. The British and Egyptians had helped write the first **constitution**. It was unclear about two important questions. First, would the new country be Islamic? Second, would Sudan allow regions some independence?

CHAPTER FOUR

Civil Wars and Terror

Sudan became an independent country on January 1, 1956. But bad news came with the good news. Civil war broke out in the new country. The cause of the war was the north-south split. The northerners had power. Southerners felt they would never have much say in the new country. They believed independence for the south was the only answer.

DIVISIONS WITHIN DIVISIONS

Sudan's problems go beyond north-south differences. They go deeper than Muslim and non-Muslim splits. In the north, for example, town and country people disagree on many issues. And the south has many different groups. These groups disagree on many things. Southerners as a group cannot even agree on what they want. Some want total independence. Others want more freedom within a united Sudan.

Drought and hunger add to the hardships that families face in southern Sudan.

BATTLE LINES

A series of governments ruled Sudan from 1956 through the mid-1960s. The army was always present. Either they were fighting southern rebels or taking over government. Sudan remained unstable and peace seemed far away.

Colonel Gafaar Muhammad Nimeiri seized power in 1969. Unlike other leaders, he agreed to talk to southern rebels. That talking led to a peace agreement in 1972. It was a rare time of peace for Sudan.

THE "MAY REVOLUTION"

By the late 1960s, Sudan had gone through many governments. But the country still had some of the same problems. Sudan still needed a strong constitution. The civil war still raged.

On May 25, 1969, Colonel Gafaar Muhammad Nimeiri and a group of army officers seized power in Sudan. The Sudanese call this the "May Revolution." Nimeiri believed his new government would be strong. It would make tough decisions. For example, it would consider independence for the south. It would reduce Muslim control of Sudanese society. Nimeiri believed this would make southerners feel part of the country.

Colonel Gafaar Muhammad Nimeiri sought peace with Sudan's neighbors and its own southern rebels in the 1970s.

THE ADDIS ABABA AGREEMENT

Sudan's civil war raged for nearly twenty years. The army expected a victory in 1970. But southern rebels fought back. And then rival rebel forces united for the first time under General Joseph Lagu. He began talks with the government to stop the fighting. In March 1972, Lagu and Colonel Nimeiri signed a peace pact in Addis Ababa, Ethiopia. The fighting ended almost overnight. The pact established a Southern Region of Sudan. This region had some self-government. It had its own lawmaking body. The Addis Ababa Agreement brought peace for eleven years.

Peace lasted until 1983. During that time, Nimeiri made new Muslim laws. Some of these offended non-Muslims. Again, war broke out. The government found itself fighting the newly formed Sudan People's Liberation Army (SPLA). The Sudan People's Liberation Movement (SPLM), the political wing of the SPLA, wanted more independence for the south. This time, the stakes were higher. The south had discovered oil. People there felt that they should get the money that came from it.

Meanwhile, extreme Muslim groups were growing in the country. Some of these groups were violent. They fought against anyone who disagreed with them. Sudan with its Muslim laws and leadership was a perfect base. In 1989, Omar al-Bashir became Sudan's new leader. He supported terrorists. Sudan was becoming a dangerous place.

Omar al-Bashir has linked Sudan with Islamic extremists since coming to power in 1989.

People in the south have supported the SPLM and SPLA as a way of having a greater voice in Sudan as a whole.

BIN LADEN IN SUDAN

In 1989, Brigadier-General Omar al-Bashir took over the Sudanese government (see page 27). Sudan began welcoming Islamic extremists from other countries. One of these was Osama Bin Laden. Bin Laden's al Qaeda group later directed the 9/11 terrorist attacks on the United States. Al Qaeda and other groups gave the government money. In return, they got a safe place to live. At their camps, they trained volunteers and gathered weapons.

This poster of Osama Bin Laden was found in an al Qaeda training center in Sudan.

U.S. missiles destroyed the El-Shifa chemical factory in Khartoum in August 1998. President Clinton believed the factory was building weapons for al Qaeda.

THE U.S. VIEW

" Sudan continued to serve as a meeting place, safe haven, and training hub for a number of international terrorist groups, particularly Osama Bin Laden's al Qaeda organization. . . .

U.S. State Department's "Patterns of Global Terrorism: 1998"

CHAPTER FIVE

Uncertain Peace

By 2000, civil wars had raged in Sudan for much of its forty-four-year history. The constant fighting had used much of the country's money. It had taken young men from their farms. It had destroyed farmland. Food was short. Hunger was widespread. At times, the shortage was close to a famine.

SUDAN AND THE UNITED STATES

The United States has not had an embassy in Sudan since 1996. At that time, the National Islamist Front governed Sudan. The United States did not like that Sudan was welcoming terrorists (see page 28). It did not agree that Sudan supported Iraq in the Persian Gulf War. Things between Sudan and the United States have improved. But the United States still sees Sudan as a "state sponsor of terrorism." Despite disagreements, the United States has tried to help Sudan find peace.

The very young, like this Sudanese child, often suffer the most in times of famine.

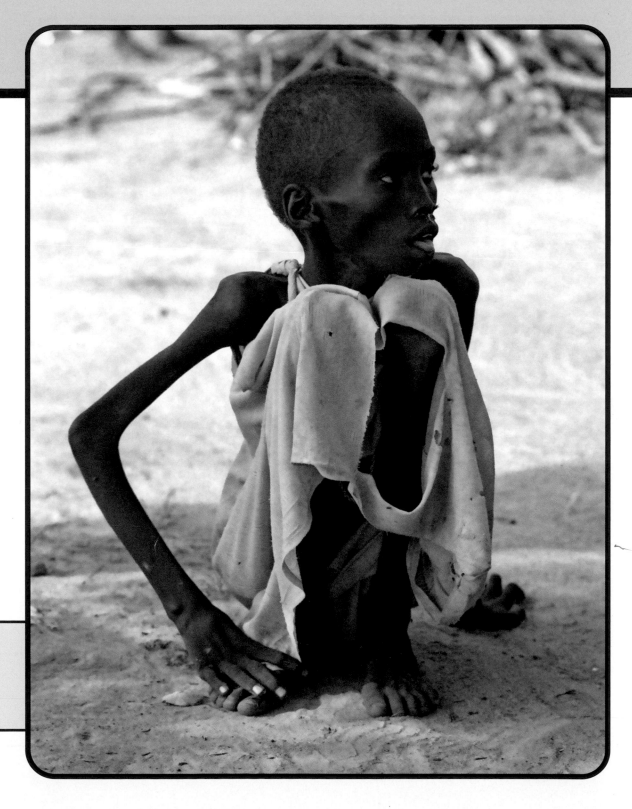

PEACE AT LAST

Sudan needed peace. Government members began to meet with southern rebel leaders. These meetings led to a peace agreement in 2002. This was the Machakos **Protocol**. This was the first step toward lasting peace in Sudan.

THE PEACE AGREEMENT

Sudan's civil war ended on January 9, 2005. That day, the Sudan government and the SPLM signed the Comprehensive Peace Agreement. It took years of discussions for these two sides to find agreement. It calls for an end to fighting. It says all government soldiers must leave southern Sudan. It also aims to return war refugees to their homes. This should be completed within six years. Then, Sudan will hold elections at all levels: president, state governors, and national and state assemblies.

SPLA members and other rebels stopped fighting while peace talks continued in Sudan.

The peace agreement took several years to complete. During that time, the fighting stopped. The final peace plan spelled out how much independence the south should have. It called for sharing Sudan's wealth between north and south. It even talked of better relations between Muslims and non-Muslims. Everything was looking good.

UN Secretary-General Kofi Annan (right) met SPLM leader John Garang on a trip to Sudan in May 2005.

PASSAGE FROM THE NEW CONSTITUTION

> The Republic of Sudan. . .is committed to the respect and promotion of human dignity and founded on **justice**, equality and the advancement of human rights and freedoms. It is an all-embracing homeland wherein races and cultures coalesce [come together] and religions co-exist in harmony.

The opening of the interim constitution of Sudan. It applies during the six-year interim period arising from the Comprehensive Peace Agreement of 2005.

CHAPTER SIX

Darfur And Beyond

In 2003, Sudan's civil war was nearly over. But the people of Sudan never celebrated. The conflict in Darfur began.

People in Darfur, like most in the north of Sudan, are Muslim. But unlike most people in the north, they are not Arab. They felt that the government was ignoring their needs. Two rebel groups, the Justice and Equality Movement (JEM) and the Sudan Liberation Movement (SLM), began protesting for the non-Arab people.

Darfur refugees cross a dried-up stream into neighboring Chad to escape violence in their own villages.

DRIVEN OFF BY WAR

Violence in Sudan has forced many Sudanese from their homes. As many as 350,000 Sudanese refugees are living in five neighboring countries. Another two million people had fled within Sudan itself. Many of these people feel that they cannot return. Their way of life in southern Sudan has been destroyed. Villages have been burned. Wells have been poisoned. Farms have almost turned into desert. Until the region can rebuild, millions of people struggle to survive.

In response to the rebel groups, the government armed local Arab **militia**. These gunmen were not the official army. But it was their job to deal with the rebels. These armed groups are called

The government allows these African Union peacekeepers into Sudan but refuses to have peacekeepers from the United Nations.

the Janjaweed. For years, these gunmen terrorized the region.

Hundreds of thousands of people have died in the fighting. Millions more have become refugees. Some have fled to Chad. Others stayed in Sudan. Those left in the Darfur area face hunger, disease—and worse.

INTERNATIONAL RESPONSE

The world has watched the events in Darfur with horror. In other troubled places, peacekeeping forces have helped to stop fighting. But the people fighting must agree to let the outsiders enter their region or country.

This has not happened in Darfur. The United Nations (UN) has offered to send in peacekeepers. But the Sudanese government has refused. It does not trust many other countries. It accuses the UN of interference.

On April 29, 2007, demonstrators in London, England (and 35 capitals around the world) marked the fourth anniversary of the Darfur conflict. They called for action and protection for the Darfur region of Sudan.

WHO CAN BRING PEACE?

The United Nations has sent peacekeeping soldiers to 61 parts of the world in the last 58 years. Some of these peacekeeping missions have helped to end violence in a region. Such a return to peace allows people to get back to normal. But both sides in a conflict must agree to have UN peacekeepers involved. In the case of Darfur, the Sudan government refuses. It has, however, allowed peacekeepers from other African countries into Darfur. Since 2004, about 7,000 soldiers from the African Union (AU) have tried to reduce fighting in Darfur. This group is far too small. Things almost changed in November 2006. The Sudan government seemed to agree to a combined United Nations/AU peace force. Within days, though, Sudan's President Bashir said that "talk of joint forces is a lie."

African Union peacekeepers remain the only outside forces to control the violence in Darfur.

POINTING THE FINGER

"We concluded that **genocide** has been committed in Darfur and that the government and the Janjaweed bear responsibility and genocide may still be occurring."

Former U.S. Secretary of State Colin Powell speaking in the U.S. Senate.

BLOCKING AID

Amnesty International tries to end unfair suffering. It called attention to Darfur's problems in 2006. More than three million people rely on help from the outside world. This help comes as food, seeds for crops, clothing, and shelter. But the fighting in the region makes it hard for this help to reach the people. Also, the Sudan government does not trust many foreign organizations. Very few aid workers are allowed into the area. Some of those allowed in have been attacked. Several have died. Darfur remains a dangerous place.

Children play by a water pump in a settlement built by the United Nations for returning refugees.

In 2006, the world considered forcing Sudan to accept peacekeepers. One idea is to refuse to trade with Sudan until the government changes its mind. Sudan relies heavily on oil sales. This might work if countries refused to buy Sudan's oil. But the Sudanese government of Sudan has a very important friend—China. They buy much of Sudan's oil and do not like the idea of stopping trade with Sudan.

This problem must be solved. Until it is, Sudan will remain a country in crisis.

TIMELINE

SUDAN

GEOGRAPHY

Area: 963,233 square miles (2,505,810 sq km)

Borders: Central African Republic, Chad, Democratic Republic of the Congo, Egypt, Eritrea, Ethiopia, Kenya, Libya, Uganda

Terrain: Mainly a flat plain with desert in the north and mountains in the northeast, far south, and west

Highest point: Kinyeti, 10,453 feet (3,187 meters)

Resources: Petroleum, iron ore, copper, chromium ore, zinc, tungsten, hydropower

Major rivers: Nile, Atbara, Gash

SOCIETY

Population (2006): 41,661,200   **Ethnic groups:** Black 52%, Arab 39%, Bema 6%, Other 3%

Languages: Arabic (official language); Nubian; Ta Bedawie; Nilotic; Nilo-Hamitic; English

Literacy: 61%

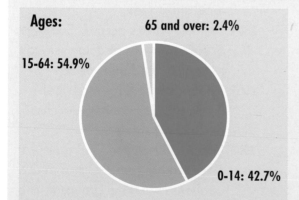

Ages:
- 65 and over: 2.4%
- 15-64: 54.9%
- 0-14: 42.7%

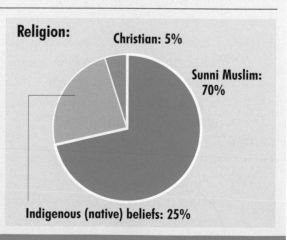

Religion:
- Christian: 5%
- Sunni Muslim: 70%
- Indigenous (native) beliefs: 25%

GOVERNMENT

Type: Republic   **Capital:** Khartoum   **States:** 25

Independence: January 1, 1956

Law: English common law and Islamic law

Vote: Universal — 17 years of age

System: President (head of government and state: elected directly every 5 years); 450-seat House of Representatives (appointed now but subject to six-year electoral terms when new constitution takes effect), 50-seat Council of States (2 representatives per state, also to elected every 6 years)

ECONOMY

Currency: Sudanese dinar

Total value of goods and services (2005): $86 billion

Labor force (2005): 11 million

Poverty (2004): 40% of the population below poverty line

Main industries (2005): oil, cotton and textiles, cement, soap distilling, edible oils, petroleum refining, pharmaceuticals

Foreign debt (2005): $27 billion

Sectors of industry (2003):

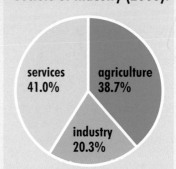

services 41.0%
agriculture 38.7%
industry 20.3%

COMMUNICATIONS AND MEDIA

Telephones (2004): 670,000 fixed line; 1.8 million mobile   **Internet users (2005):** 1.1 million

TV stations: 3

Newspapers: 13, in Arabic except for Khartoum Monitor (in English) and Post (English)

Radio: 14 stations (including local stations broadcasting in AM, FM, and short wave)

Airports: 88   **Railways:** 3,706 miles (5,978 km)   **Roads:** 7,378 miles (11,900 km)

Ships: 2 over 1,102 tons (1000 tonnes)   **Ports:** Port Sudan

MILITARY

Branches: Army, Navy, Air Force, popular defense force

Service: compulsory for 3 years between the ages of 18 and 30

GLOSSARY

civil war (SIV il wor) — conflict between two or more groups within a country

colony (KOL uh nee) — region ruled by a powerful foreign country, often far away

concentration camp (KON suhn tray shuhn kamp) — harsh prison used in wartime

constitution (kon stuh TOO shuhn) — written document stating how an organization or country should be run

ethnic group (ETH nik groop) — people who share appearance or background

genocide (JEN uh side) — the deliberate killing of a group of people because of their nationality or beliefs

justice (JUHSS tiss) — treatment that is fair and morally right

Islam (i SLAHM) — the belief in one God (Allah) as revealed to the prophet Muhammad

militia (muh LISH uh) — people trained as soldiers but not part of a regular army

Muslim (MUHZ luhm) — follower of the religion of Islam

parliament (PAR luh muhnt) — a group of elected people who define the laws of a country

protocol (PROH tuh kuhl) — the first copy of a treaty before it has been officially agreed

rape (rape) — forcing a person to have sex against her will

refugee (ref yuh JEE) — someone who flees from an area because of fighting or natural disaster

tribute (TRIB yoot) — money or goods paid to a conqueror

tropical (TROP uh kuhl) — having hot and wet weather for most of the year

FURTHER INFORMATION

WEBSITES

BBC Country Profile: Sudan

http://news.bbc.co.uk/1/hi/country_profiles

This site has timelines, background stories, links, and updates.

CIA Factbook

https://www.cia.gov/library/publications/the-world-factbook

A comprehensive store of facts and statistics on Sudan.

The Cyberschoolbus

www.un.org/cyberschoolbus

This is the children's section of the United Nations website. It has profiles of Sudan, the Darfur conflict, and relief and peacekeeping efforts.

BOOKS

Brothers in Hope: The Story of the Lost Boys of Sudan. Mary Williams. Lee & Low Books, 2005.

Genocide. Jane Springer. Groundwood Books, 2006.

Sudan in Pictures (Virtual Geography series). Francesca Davis DiPiazza. Twenty-First Century Books, 2006.

The Lost Boys of Sudan: An American Story of the Refugee Experience. Mark Bixler. University of Georgia Press, 2006.

INDEX